Lilu makes Laddoos

by Devika Joglekar

Lilu makes Laddoos ©

Text and Art copyright © by Devika Joglekar 2018

Published by Miheika Publications

Email: info@miheika.com
URL: www.miheika.com

ISBN-13: 978-1981256242
ISBN-10: 1981256245

Dedicated to kids(of all ages) with a sweet tooth.

Here comes the festival of lights...
Diwali!

Hi! I am Lilu. Big sister of Little Kuku.

Little Kuku wants me
to give him a Diwali gift.

Probably not a big football like last year,
which he couldn't even lift!

Hmm... Let's see. What would he like?

I know! Little Kuku likes to eat.
Maybe I should make him a yummy treat!

But Mom has already made so many sweets. Now, what else can I do?

Wait! I don't see Little Kuku's favorite laddoo*.

*An Indian sweet

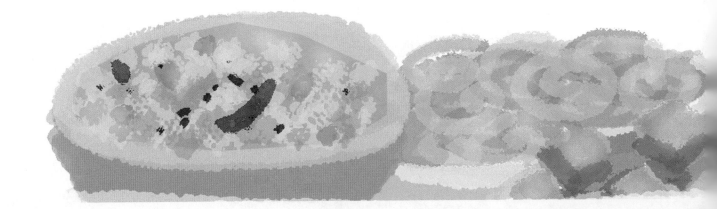

For laddoos, I would need sugar, raisins, ghee*, cardamom powder and lots of gram flour.

Mom said,"Let me help you, that way, we'll finish making them in an hour!"

*ghee is Indian clarified butter.

First, place the pan on the stove
and add the ghee.

Wait till it melts. Don't rush!
While cooking, patience is the key!

Now we add the gram flour to the ghee, and stir it well till it turns golden brown.

While Mom is helping, I fancy myself wearing a chef's crown!

The color has changed and
it smells so good!

Now let's take it off the stove and
let it cool.

Add the sugar, raisins, and mix it well.

If I am forgetting anything, please do tell!

Wait! We need to add the cardamom powder.
How can I forget?

It adds to the taste, you can bet!

Now take some of that mixture and mould it into a laddoo, big and round!

Be careful not to leave a mess around!

How about adding cashews as garnish?
Good idea!

Now that's a finish!

Yippee! All done!

Watching the joy on Little Kuku's face will be fun.

Next thing I need is a box
to gift-pack.

Let me go and see if I can find
something on the big rack.

The box of laddoos is ready!

Yay! I have a wrapping paper which has pictures of a teddy.

Tonight is Diwali!
Wherever I see, there is light.

Little Kuku must be in the kitchen, looking for a small bite!

"Mommy! You forgot to make my favorite laddoos?" Little Kuku cried.

Hehehe!
He's about to be surprised.

Look, Little Kuku!
Here is your favorite laddoo!

He was so happy that he gave me a kiss.
And a hug too!

Little Kuku had some of the laddoos...
not one or two, but three!

I am so glad that I can't hide my glee.

Little Kuku said that the laddoos were full of goodness, in every bite.

We wish you all a very Happy Diwali, full of light!

Besan/Gram Flour Laddoos recipe

You need:

| 1 cup Gram Flour/ Besan | 1/4 cup Clarified Butter | 1/2 cup Powdered Sugar |

1. Heat a thick bottom pan and add the ghee.

1/4 tsp
Powdered
Cardamom

10 - 15
Raisins

Cashews

2. Once the ghee melts, add the gram flour and mix it well.

3. On a low flame, stir continuously for 25-30 mins till the flour color changes to golden brown.

4. Take it off the flame and allow it to cool completely.

5. Add sugar, cardamom powder, raisins and mix it well.

6. Take around 1 tbsp of the prepared mixture and mould it into a round laddoo, with your hands.

7. Garnish each laddoo with a cashew.

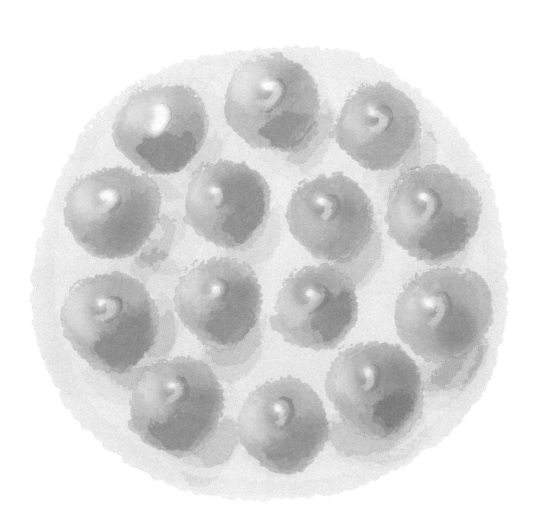

Children's books by Miheika Publications
Visit: www.miheika.com

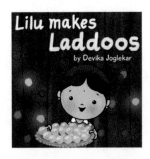
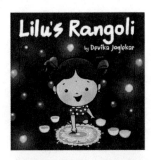
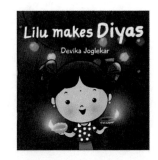

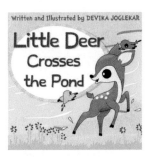
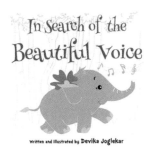

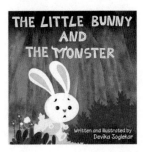

Devika Joglekar is an animator and illustrator. She has always aspired to author children's books, which are not only fun to read but also inspire young readers to learn and discover interesting things.

She has been bringing ideas to life through her labor of love, miheika.com.

Originally from India, she now lives with her husband in San Francisco Bay Area.